MW01153919

COUNTING ON CARIBOU

Text by
Patricia H. Partnow, PhD

Illustrations by
Diana Magnuson

muddy boots™

we jump in puddles

Guilford, Connecticut

It was a Monday in February. Fifth-grader Bruce Turner squirmed in his seat. It was -20 degrees outside and a blizzard was burying streets and driving the snow against doorways. There had been no outdoor recess today. Bruce was bored. He wanted to be outside where he spent hours year-round, following animal tracks, observing snow geese during nesting season, finding tuttu antlers on the tundra, watching gulls and ravens soar overhead in the wind, and jigging for fish under the river ice. Bruce thought his village, Nuiqsut, was the best place in the world because he could do all the things he loved right here. But for now, Bruce was inside in the classroom getting ready for a visit by an elder, George Reilly, who would tell ancient stories called **unipkaat** about **tuttut.** A few minutes later, Shirley, Bruce's teacher, welcomed George to the classroom.

3

George peered at the class through his bifocals and cleared his throat. "Ah, tuttut!" he said. "Yes, I know some unipkaat about tuttut. I'll tell you one that every Iñupiaq should know, because our lives depend on it."

"You know why the tuttut keep coming back for us to hunt? It's because of a deal our ancestors made with them long, long ago. It was thanks to one tuttut that we know how to show respect to them."

4

Like the rest of the kids in the class, Bruce knew how to behave when an elder told an **unipkaaq,** or in fact any kind of story. They would listen politely. They would not fidget or interrupt, though one or two of them might say, **"ii!"** every now and then to let the elder know they understood and appreciated the story. As George began telling his story, Bruce leaned toward the elder to catch every word. His eyes widened.

"Long, long ago," George continued, *"a good hunter had bad luck with the tuttut. It was because his wife had become careless with the meat. She tossed the heads onto the ground as if they were trash and allowed dirt to get into the lifeless eyes. The tuttut became frightened of the hunter. Even though he went out every day to look for food, he was not successful.*

"Then one day when he was out on the tundra a stranger came up to him. The stranger looked like a man, but his heart was outside of his chest, swinging as if on a string."
'George continued, "It turned out this man was the chief tuttu in human form. He explained that his separate heart meant that he could not be killed even if the rest of his body died — but he and his fellow tuttut could still choose to stay away from people who did not respect them.

"'Your wife has to change,' the chief tuttu told the man. 'No more complaining, no throwing the meat or heads around.' The man rushed back to his sod house. His wife listened and changed her disrespectful ways.

"This was the bargain between people and tuttut that we still follow today to be sure the tuttut keep coming back to be hunted."*

As George finished his story, several of the students sighed in satisfaction. *"Aa!"* several of them breathed, acknowledging a well-told story.

*A retelling of "The Chief of the Caribou" as told by Elijah Kakinya in Nunamiut Unipkaaŋich.

The next day, Kathy Reilly, George's wife, came to class. She was Nunamiu, an inland Iñupiaq from the other side of the Brooks Range. She told an ***uqaluktuaq***, a history story, about the time when the caribou disappeared from their homeland, and her grandparents had to move to the coast where they could get food from the sea and goods from White traders.

It was around 1900. Whalers from New England were already here, and they were joined by gold seekers. The new arrivals hunted the tuttut for both meat and the hides, because caribou fur is the warmest for parkas. Its hollow hairs trap air and provide excellent insulation against the cold.

Meanwhile, the traders on the coast encouraged the Nunamiut to bring them more and more tuttu skins to clothe the whalers and meat to feed them. The tuttu herd became smaller and smaller. Finally, there were so few tuttut that people started going hungry. Most of the Nunamiut moved north to the coast.

Kathy finished her *uqaluktuaq* by reassuring the class that the caribou had come back to the mountains. When the whalers and gold seekers left, the numbers of tuttut increased. By the 1930s, the Nunamiut knew they could move back to the Brooks Range.

9

As he walked home from school that afternoon, Bruce scanned the flat horizon, looking upriver in the glow of the full moon in the direction of the mountains. His sharp eyes immediately noticed movement far away. Five tiny silhouettes shuffled slowly from left to right on the tundra, their heads down. Even so, he could see antlers on one of them. Definitely tuttut! Bruce could even make out a pawing motion as they scraped the snow away looking for lichen to eat. His heart raced. He knew his father would take him hunting if he hurried home.

10

When he got home,
Bruce's dad, Jimmy, was
packing the snowmachine
sled with survival gear, two rifles, and
ammunition. "You better hurry," Jimmy said.
"Get your gear on so we can get to those
caribou before they go away."

Even as he rushed along to pack his gear, in the back
of his mind Bruce had a guilty feeling that he
took caribou for granted. Way back in the
past, would the chief of the tuttut have
punished him for not being grateful
enough?

Unlike the old days, Bruce had never known true hunger. There had always been caribou meat in his family's ice cellar waiting to be cooked into a soup or stew or eaten frozen raw as tuttu quaq. But after hearing the stories from George and Kathy, he wondered if he could count on the meat being available whenever he wanted it in the future.

Their hunt was successful, yielding one young male tuttu. After gutting it, they tied the carcass to the snowmachine sled and headed back to the village. Bruce's aaka had asked them not to quarter the caribou. She wanted to harvest the backstrap to make *ivalu,* or sinew, for her skin sewing projects.

That night over supper, the family was careful to give thanks for the hunt. Then Bruce asked his dad, "Why are the tuttut here sometimes and sometimes nowhere near?"

Jimmy responded, "They migrate to the coast, just west of Nuiqsut, every summer, and a few stay on the coast during winter. But most of them head south into the hills and mountains in the fall. You can see their trails on the tundra. In just one migration, if there are hundreds in the herd, the ground gets worn into a clear path – and the path stays visible for several years. So when I go on a hunt for tuttut, I just follow the migration routes." Jimmy paused a minute before adding, "But you can't count on the caribou to follow the exact same route every year. You have to pay attention and share information with other hunters."

"How can we be sure the caribou won't disappear, like they did long ago when people didn't treat them right? Or like when they were overhunted in 1900?" Bruce persisted.

"Good question," Jimmy answered. "I'll pass that one to your mom."

Bruce's mother Bernice was the information officer for the village subsistence office. She said, "I think it's time to show your teacher and the other students some facts about tuttut."

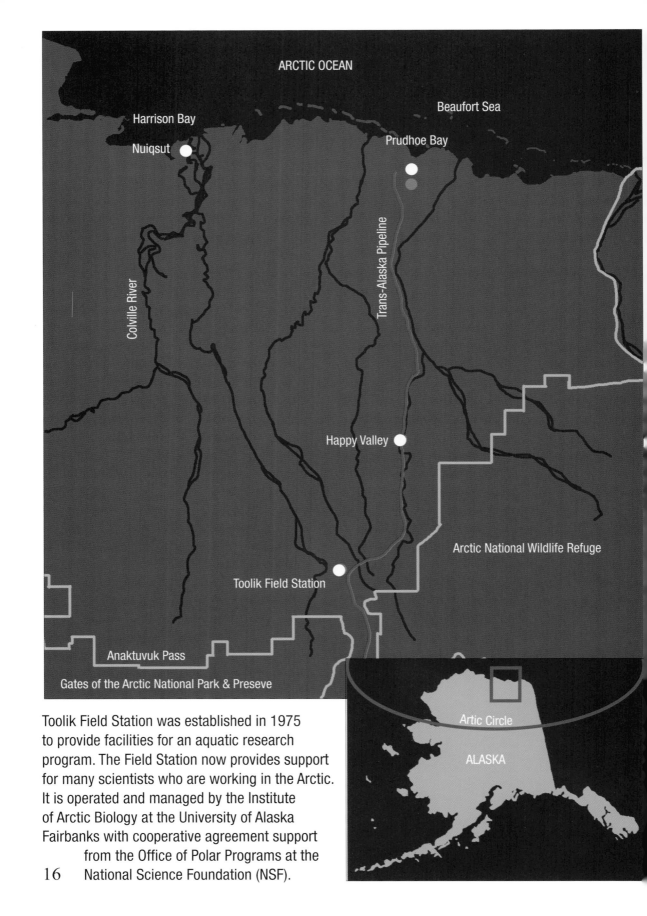

ARCTIC OCEAN

Beaufort Sea

Harrison Bay

Prudhoe Bay

Nuiqsut

Trans-Alaska Pipeline

Colville River

Happy Valley

Arctic National Wildlife Refuge

Toolik Field Station

Anaktuvuk Pass

Gates of the Arctic National Park & Preseve

Artic Circle

ALASKA

Toolik Field Station was established in 1975 to provide facilities for an aquatic research program. The Field Station now provides support for many scientists who are working in the Arctic. It is operated and managed by the Institute of Arctic Biology at the University of Alaska Fairbanks with cooperative agreement support from the Office of Polar Programs at the

National Science Foundation (NSF).

When it was time for social studies and science the next day, Bruce was surprised to see his mother come into the classroom. She grinned at Bruce as Shirley said, "Special treat! Mrs. Turner has come from the village subsistence office."

Bernice took two large maps and some papers from a cardboard tube she had carried in. She spread them on the table and the students gathered around. "These maps show where the caribou live and move near Nuiqsut. This one is from last year when our village council worked with biologists from Toolik Lake to count and track them. The other one is from 35 years ago when I was your age." She pointed to a large colorful graph, and said, "And these graphs show how many caribou Nuiqsut hunters got last year, compared to how many they got 35 years ago. What do you notice when you compare the maps and graphs?"

"Thirty-five years ago, a lot of us had snowmachines but not every family had an ATV," she continued. "And 35 years ago, Nuiqsut had only about half as many people as we have today. So pressure on the caribou is greater now than it was then."

Shirley then asked the question that had been on Bruce's mind. "Mrs. Turner, I'm wondering if people of your generation still follow the old rules about treating caribou respectfully."

"Some do," Bernice answered. "We do in our family. But I know not everyone does. Some of the younger people never learned from their elders because they went away to school when they were teenagers. Others maybe forgot or got a little lazy about the old customs because it was so easy to shoot and retrieve. They focused on becoming proficient hunters rather than good hunters."

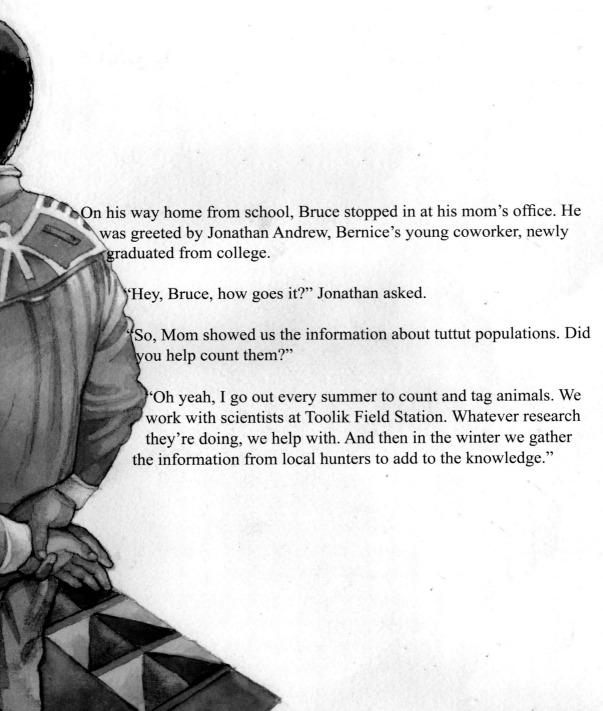

On his way home from school, Bruce stopped in at his mom's office. He was greeted by Jonathan Andrew, Bernice's young coworker, newly graduated from college.

"Hey, Bruce, how goes it?" Jonathan asked.

"So, Mom showed us the information about tuttut populations. Did you help count them?"

"Oh yeah, I go out every summer to count and tag animals. We work with scientists at Toolik Field Station. Whatever research they're doing, we help with. And then in the winter we gather the information from local hunters to add to the knowledge."

"So, how do you count the tuttut? My dad and I went upriver one time and I saw a HUGE herd. How can you possibly count them all? They go by so fast!"

Jonathan opened his desk drawer and pulled out a metal counter that fit neatly in his hand. "See this? Every time I click it a number advances. And I click it every time a tuttu goes by an imaginary line I draw between myself and some distant feature, like a stone outcrop. I gotta tell you, my thumb gets tired after a day of clicking!"

"How old do you have to be to go on one of those counting trips?" Bruce asked.

"Well, it's not just counting, it's observing and tagging too. Usually the research assistants are college kids, but I don't see why a high school kid couldn't do it too. Give it a few years, keep hunting with your dad, and come back to ask us when you're in ninth grade." Bruce's face collapsed. "That's almost four years from now!" he moaned. Jonathan smiled, shook his head, and said, "Go play. Have some fun!"

Bruce left, but he didn't play. Instead, he shuffled his feet in the dirt as he slowly walked home. "Why should we leave everything up to the grownups?" Bruce huffed. "Why can't I go out with the scientists this summer to help count the tuttut? Why can't I see for myself how healthy the animals look, and whether all the females having calves?" He decided he had to find a way to get a spot on the tuttu counting crew this summer. The problem was, he had no idea how to convince his mother and Jonathan to let him go.

As he often did when he had a problem, he went to his ***aaka*** for advice.

"Well, Tutiiŋ," she said, "when I was a little girl my father would never let me go hunting. He always took my brother, but not me. He said I would be a burden and would not know what to do out there. So when my dad and brother were hunting one winter I went out on my own every day for two weeks, and snared a bunch of hare and ptarmigan. I gave the meat to my mom, who treated me just like a boy: she shared my catches with everyone else in our little settlement. Then when my father and brother got back from their trip, I brought out a whole bundle of furs and feathered pelts. My father said, 'You did this?' 'Iii!' I answered. From then on he let me go with him."

Bruce pondered how he could prove himself to the grownups as his aaka had done. Soon he had a plan, but it would take the rest of the school year to complete. That night over dinner, he said to his mother, "Jonathan told me they let students go on the summer tuttu count. I want to go this summer."

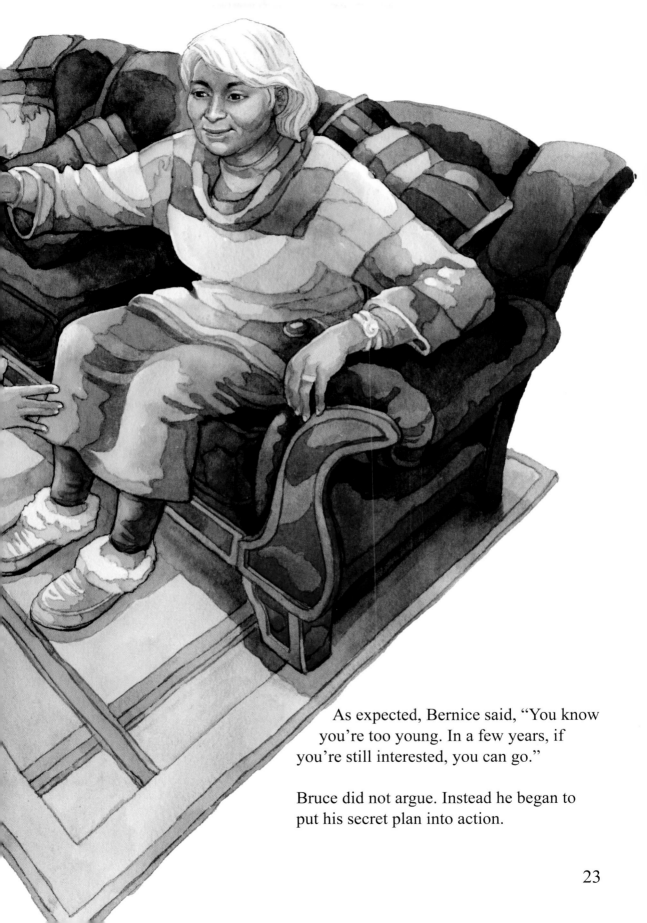

As expected, Bernice said, "You know you're too young. In a few years, if you're still interested, you can go."

Bruce did not argue. Instead he began to put his secret plan into action.

23

It was actually very simple: first, he would demonstrate what a hard worker he was. He chopped wood every day, delivering it not just to his own house and his aaka's, but to other elderly people in the village as well. He helped his parents clean out the ice cellar without being asked. He cleaned a winter's worth of debris from around the house. One day as he was delivering wood to George and Kathy Reilly, he overheard George through the open window. "That boy knows how to show respect!" Bruce grinned as he stacked the wood.

Next, Bruce planned to show that he understood basic machinery, in case anyone's vehicle had problems during the counting trip. He cleaned the spark plugs on the village subsistence office's Argo. He changed the oil. He checked the filters. He cleaned and oiled the chains.

Seven weeks later, summer was well on its way. Spring whaling had come and gone, a successful year. Three crews had taken whales and the whole village was sharing in the bounty. Days were getting long, nights short. In a month, the sun would set for a few hours, then stay up continuously for the next two-and-a-half months. The students found it harder and harder to concentrate on classwork. The constant drip of melting snow, warnings not to venture out onto the softening ice, the coming of the snow buntings, and patches of bare tundra signaled to all that summer preparations needed to be completed very soon.

It was time to put into action the third part of Bruce's plan. He would show his knowledge and skills at camping and coping outside of the village. This task was the trickiest, because he had to get his parents' permission to spend a weekend out on the tundra with a friend. He promised to take the two-way radio and showed that he knew how to use it. He had his parents inspect his survival bag, which contained flares, waterproof matches, newly patched rubber boots, and other necessities. He packed food, a pot, his rifle, and ammunition.

Just before leaving, Bruce pulled out a laminated map and showed his parents exactly where he and his friend would go. Then the two 11-year olds set out on a bright Friday afternoon, promising to return by Sunday before dinner. The snowmachine engine drowned out his father's last bit of advice: "Watch the clouds and wind. Remember what we've taught you!" and his mother, "Have fun. Pay attention to what you see!"

Binoculars, counter, knife, knife sharpener, flashlight, headlamp, utility tool, radios, GPS, survival tool, dry bag, water bottles, space blanket, fire starting kit, bear spray, food bag, sleeping bag, boots.

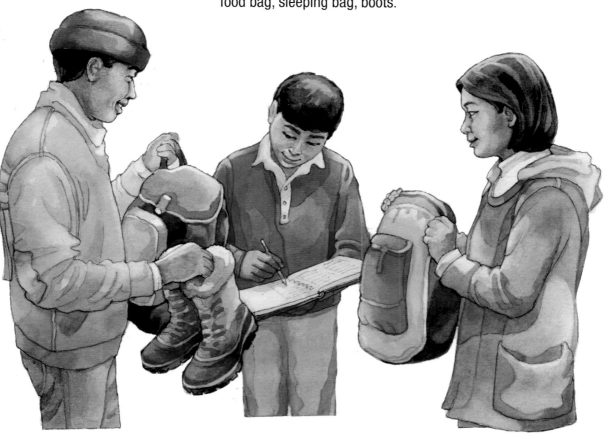

Zip Lock bags, electrical & duct tape, personal gear including toothbrush, lip balm, sunglasses, sunscreen, pain relievers, medication. Clothing; underlayer, shirt, pants, insulated outerwear, rainwear, headware, socks, insulated gloves.

By the beginning of May, Bruce's plan had been carried out. School was almost done for the year and he thought the subsistence office must be making its final plans for summer fieldwork. After school on May 4 he strode into his mom's office to make his pitch. He explained that he knew how to work hard, how to fix things, and how to live outside on his own. He finished with, "I think I can help on the fieldtrip. I'll do whatever you want: cook, pack, guard the camp. And I can count tuttut."

Bernice and Jonathan were respectfully silent for a moment before his mom said, "Bruce, I know you've been working hard, but it's not our decision. We met with the folks at Toolik Lake two months ago to plan the season. All the spots on the team are filled. Even if you were old enough, which you aren't, there's no room for you. I'm sorry."

Bruce was crushed. He turned abruptly and pushed on the door as he barreled outside. He muttered, "No matter what I do, I can't get them to let me go! That shows how much Aaka knows!"

Head down, he trudged the hundred yards to the school, then stumbled up the steps and into the building. The steady thump of a dribbling basketball and squeaks of sneakers on the gym floor greeted him, but he ignored the sounds and went straight to the library. As he passed through the doorway, he glanced at the display case to his right. He would have missed the one piece of information he needed if it had not been written in big red letters beneath the picture of a tuttu. It was a notice from the Toolik Field Station researchers to the students of Nuiqsut Trapper School.

The notice said,

> 'We can take one teenager who can get along outdoors and who wants to apprentice in our caribou study this year. This is a last-minute vacancy, caused by the sudden departure of one of our workers who went on maternity leave earlier than anticipated. Write us by May 5 telling about your qualifications.'

Bruce let out a yelp. Yes! The chance he needed! And the deadline was tomorrow. No time to waste. He ignored the fact that he was not yet a teenager, feeling confident that his skills and interests would secure him a spot on the team.

Bruce began typing on one of the library computers. His letter repeated the pitch he had made to his mother and Jonathan. After he finished, he found Shirley in her classroom preparing for the next day's lessons, and asked her to read his draft. She took the paper and read it with raised eyebrows. She corrected the spelling of two words and made a few suggestions on wording, and then asked, "But aren't you too young?" Bruce just smiled. "I might be young but I think I'm the right person for this."

In the end, Bruce was chosen to go. Jonathan promised to look after him during the summer, but no one was worried about Bruce's behavior or ability to do well at camp. After all, he had been hunting and camping with his family all his life.

Once out in the field, Bruce shared in most of the camp chores. He helped set up tents and latrines. He was scheduled as part of the clean-up rotation. He was given a caribou counter and instructions on how to use it. He fished for the crew's dinner.

After observing the scientists for a week, he was even allowed to help fit tracking collars and take blood samples from darted caribou. However, due to his youth, he was spared some jobs that were restricted to the grownups. For instance, he was relieved of cooking detail after his first attempt to make oatmeal resulted in large gummy globs of mush that no one would eat. Instead, he was tasked with cleaning up all traces of leftovers after meals and making sure the food was secured in bear-proof canisters. And, though he proclaimed that he was willing to be on the bear- and wolf-watch detail during both day and night, the team leaders decided that job was better left to the adults.

Bruce's favorite part of the day was when he watched and counted the tuttut. The first day in the field, he had been handed a waterproof notebook for his observations, and Jonathan coached him on what he should include: the behavior of cows with their calves, herd movement, attacks by predators such as bears and wolves. He was to write descriptions of caribou activities, such as jumping around and snorting, behavior that would show they were trying to avoid flies and mosquitoes. He was told to write about interactions among young tuttut and aggression between adult males. His notebook was nearly full by the end of the trip.

Bruce and Jonathan returned to the village in early August. After hugging his mom and dad, Bruce grabbed a piece of smoked fish, dipped it in seal oil, and popped it into his mouth. "Ahh!" he moaned as he chewed, eyes closed. "That's what I'm talking about!" Next, Bruce took a long, hot shower and put on clean clothes. He hopped on his bike and made a circuit around the village, reassuring himself that it looked pretty much the same as when he had left just five weeks ago, though he noticed that the teachers were returning from their summer break. He spotted Shirley lugging a plastic tote full of food and paper supplies into her apartment and stopped to help her.

"Thanks, Bruce!" she exclaimed with a smile. I understand you had quite the adventure this summer. I hear that our first school assembly will feature you, telling all about it!"

Bruce gulped. He had almost forgotten that part of the agreement with Toolik Field Station scientists – that he had to make a full report to the school, to be delivered in the fall.

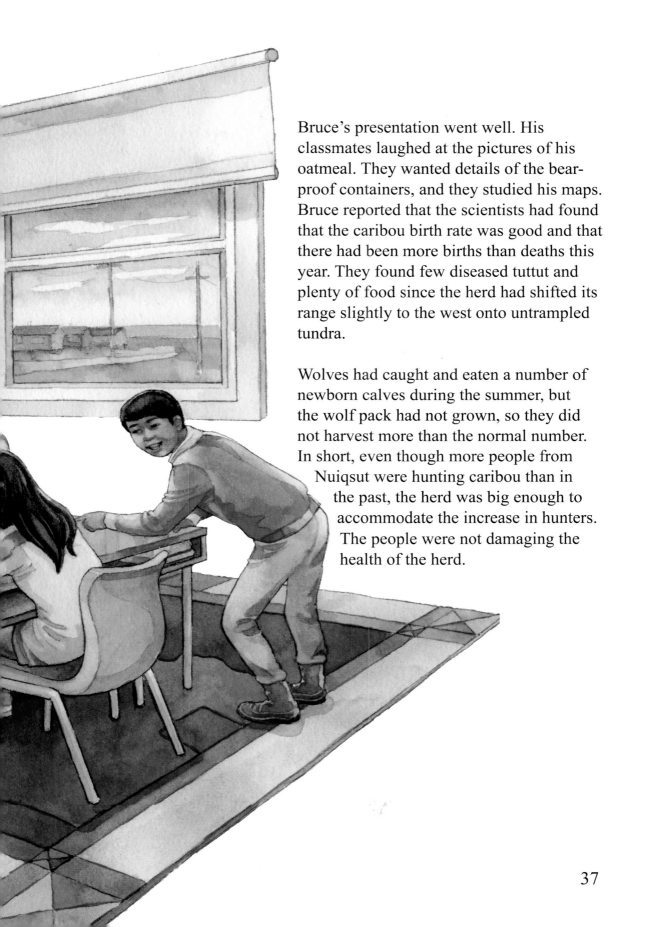

Bruce's presentation went well. His classmates laughed at the pictures of his oatmeal. They wanted details of the bear-proof containers, and they studied his maps. Bruce reported that the scientists had found that the caribou birth rate was good and that there had been more births than deaths this year. They found few diseased tuttut and plenty of food since the herd had shifted its range slightly to the west onto untrampled tundra.

Wolves had caught and eaten a number of newborn calves during the summer, but the wolf pack had not grown, so they did not harvest more than the normal number. In short, even though more people from Nuiqsut were hunting caribou than in the past, the herd was big enough to accommodate the increase in hunters. The people were not damaging the health of the herd.

In later years, Bruce would realize that the most important result of that first season in the field was a special relationship with caribou. He now saw them not just as food or even as interesting animals whose behavior he could study. It was much more intimate than that. One evening stood out in his memory as a sign of the change. While on caribou observation duty, he had seen a large bull on a hill silhouetted against the sky. He had grabbed the binoculars to get a closer look. He was sure he saw something dangling from the tuttu's chest. As the bull turned to look down from his perch toward the humans below, Bruce had felt sure the animal was singling him out. The responsibility for telling future generations about the special relationship between inuk and tuttu had been passed to him.

Glossary*

aaka: what people call their grandmothers nowadays, although originally it meant "mother."

ii: yes

iñua: the life force or spirit of an animal, plant, geographic feature; the sensate being the lies within them.

inuk: person

Iñupiaq (plural, Iñupiat): an indigenous person from the northern and northwestern part of Alaska. The Iñupiat share a traditional language with the Inuit of northern Canada. Called "Eskimos" in the literature of the 18th, 19th, and 20th centuries, the people more accurately refer to themselves as "Iñupiat," from "inuk," meaning "person" and "piaq," meaning "real or authentic".

ivalu: sinew, used in skin sewing. The best ivalu for thread comes from the legs or back of large mammals such as caribou.

Nuiqsut: a village on the North Slope of Alaska along the banks of the Colville River, 18 miles from the Beaufort Sea.

Nunamiu (plural, Nunamiut): an Iñupiaq person from inland (from "nuna," meaning land, and "miut," meaning "people of"). The Nunamiut in this story are the people of Anaktuvuk Pass in the Brooks Range.

tutii: "my grandchild," when speaking to the child

tuttu (plural, tuttut): caribou

unipkaaq (plural, unipkaat): legend, old story, fable, or myth; a true story about the distant past that includes both physical and spiritual aspects of life.

uqaluktuaq (plural, uqaluktuat): true story or account of events that occurred within the last two or three generations.

*Iñupiaq singular nouns often end in a "q", which represents a sound similar to "k", but made further back in the mouth. Plural nouns usually end in a "t" or occasionally "ch". The word for "caribou" is a bit different: The singular is "tuttu," the dual is "tuttuk," and the plural "tuttut.

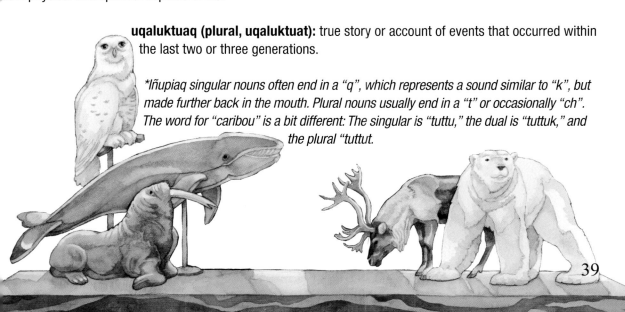

we jump in puddles

An imprint of The Rowman & Littlefield Publishing Group, Inc.
4501 Forbes Blvd., Ste. 200
Lanham, MD 20706
www.rowman.com

Distributed by NATIONAL BOOK NETWORK

British Library Cataloguing in Publication Information available

Library of Congress Cataloging-in-Publication Data available

ISBN 978-1-63076-380-0 (cloth: alk. paper)
ISBN 978-1-63076-381-7 (electronic)

Printed in Selangor Darul Ehsan Malaysia February 2020